The Poems of Eden's Eve

Amie Taylor

Published by Amie Taylor, 2024.

THE POEMS OF EDEN'S EVE

First edition. November 10, 2024.

ISBN: 979-8227301253

Written by Amie Taylor.

Poems of Eden's Eve
By
Amie Taylor

Introduction

We all have our share of feelings; some are good, and some are bad. The point is that we all have them. The best and healthiest way for me to express mine is to write them all out in poetry, so sit back, prop up your feet, and get ready to go with me on a journey of love, sadness, pain, rage, happiness, heartache, and every other human emotion. It is a book that you will relate to and enjoy.

Nothing's what it seems

With every little tear
There is a deep fear.
With every devilish grin
There is a terrible sin.
With every kiss

There is so very much you miss.
The kiss could be fake.
Even as deadly as a snake
Where there is deceit
There shall always be defeat
So be discreet with all you meet!

Torn

My soul is lost and torn.
Torn as if stabbed by a sharp thorn.
I want to scream and to shout, shout out your name
How, thanks to you, I shall never be the same.
I curse you to feel the fires of hell

To lock you up in a lonely cell.
The devil shall do to you as he desires
While you burn in his raging fires.
You will be all the other liars.
I promise you cannot hide.
Not when the devil's at your side.
There was a price I had to pay
With the devil, I, too, must stay.
I shall become his bride
When I am done with you, you'll wish you never lied!

The Beast

In the presence of the dark beast
From his golden plate, I did feast.
In the darkness, demons hide
Still, I remain at his evil side.
He is the best lover I have ever had

To be at his side, I am glad.
He fulfills my every desire.
I don't even mind the raging fire.
He shall never set me free.
In the darkness, I shall forever be.

Sin of lust

The sin of our lust
It was full of spite and disgust.
Nothing we should trust.
I thought it was love.
That it was sent from above.

Then came the killing
At first, it was thrilling.
Then it became bone-chilling.
I am in great sorrow.
There may not be a tomorrow.
I must pay for my sin.
I shall never see the grace of God again.

Lost

Lost in a World of Darkness
No one you would miss.
I have received the immortal kiss.
Caught up in his burning flame
He has played and won the game.
He promised to fulfill my desires.

He is truly the king of all liars.
The gates of hell swing open wide
There is no place to hide.
I must spend eternity by his side
I am the devil's bride.

Misery

Her true self she must forever hide
No one can ever know all the tears she's cried.
She is completely withdrawn and lost
Her heart has become cold as frost.
To her love, she holds out her hand
But he doesn't seem to understand.

Apart from one another, they have grown
She feels so utterly alone.
All they see are the lies.
On the inside, she cries.
Why can't you hear me?
I am misery!

The Musician

Inside of him, there was so much despair
For anyone, he no longer did care.
He lived his life from day to day.
In one place, he refused to stay.
Deep in the darkness, he did hide,
Never let anyone inside.
Each night, he walked out onto that stage
The only place he could release his rage.

Savage

My tender savage
My body is yours to ravage.
So, use your dark charms.
Pull me into your strong arms.
Lay me down on your feather bed
All my clothes, please shed.
With your seductive kiss
We shall enter eternal bliss.

I am the one

I am the one who is unique
Into your bed, I shall sneak.
I am the ultimate freak.
I am your one and only.
I will always be there when you're lonely.
I am your slave
Your soul only I can save.

You may be the king
but to you, I am everything.

Living dead

Nothing but dark thoughts in her head
No tears she has ever shed
No words of love have been said
She is the living dead
She walks among us
Fulfilling her bloodlust
Her heart

full of deceit and mistrust
She has come to destroy us all
to watch this world fall

Too late

Trapped deep inside yourself
as all tried to nurse you back to health.
They do not seem to see
all the pain and misery
Inside of thee.
One wonderful day
They will know all you have tried to say.
But you will have already met your fate

Their understanding came too late.

Is it real

It isn't from up above
This thing we call love.
Perhaps it is a soft caress
The unbuttoning of your dress.
I have mistaken lust for love
When push comes to shove.
It was the sly glance.

The hand slipping down your pants.
It starts the fire
That turns into a desire.
From there, love grows
who knows.
This love could heal.
Or this love can kill.
Tell me how does it make you feel
Tell me, is it fake or real?

His arms

Into his strong arms, she did fly
Together, their limit was the sky.
Together, in the end, they would die.
He won her with all of his charms
For all eternity, they shall lie in each other's arms.

Surrender

Surrender to me, my love, he said
As feathered kisses touched my head.
Please give me your body and soul
only, and then shall we be whole.
Surrender my love to only me

You know I am your destiny.

Deep within

Deep within ourselves, we all hide
We keep all our feelings bottled inside.
why do we torture ourselves so
Perhaps we should let go.
Seize the moment as it is given

and live our lives while they are still worth liven.

My whole heart

By you, my heart was taken
with me; you shall never be forsaken.
Just take my hand
by your side. I'll forever stand.
we can overcome it all
I will never let you fall.
I am you, and you are me
We are each other's destiny.

Love

when push came to shove
out of our passion grew a love
out of love grew trust
out of our trust grew so much more than common lust
we are now as one
nothing can happen to make this come undone
together, we share divine love to stand the test of time
I am forever yours, and you're forever mine

As if he had

As if to her, he had a right
he came for her in the middle of the night
it was a shocking sight
he grabbed her up into his arms
she became helpless against his charms
before she could even protest
his hands were upon her breasts
oh, what a fearful sight
this maiden and her Dark Knight

The Darkness of Night

The darkness of the night
It is a beautiful sight
So much better than the light
The burning fire is what we all desire
Our skin is white like milk
soft as the finest of silk
our lips are blood-red
no tears for you do we shed
when we give you our immortal kiss
It sends you into eternal darkness
we are vampires
only we can fulfill your desires

Lies, lies

He sat before me, looking into my eyes
he knew all he had said were lies
now, he sits alone and cries
he got a thrill each time he did lie
when caught, he would sigh
say he can't help but lie
for it is his one actual high

Forever

It is now or never
I refuse to wait forever
To this, I am clever
without you, days are Grey
I am begging you to stay
you're the reason I believe in love
for you, I think the goddess above
all my dreams came true
the night that I met you

Protection

In the mirror, I see my reflection
Goddess, grant me your protection
Protection against the love in my heart
the pain I feel when my love and I are apart
tears now fall from my eyes
I remember all of his lies
In him, I needed to believe
my heart, he did deceive
I am not sure what is real
tell me what I should feel

no matter the cost
I'm so tired of being lost

Tell me

Tell me what I should do
I have built my entire world around you
I feel so much when you touch my hand
with you, I'm in a constant wonderland
near you, my heart does dance
so I always give you another chance
for you, I cry each day
are you coming home to stay

Tonight

Tonight, you glanced my way
I was lost as to what to say
you may be the one who can save me
from this terrible misery
tonight, you touched me
I may need you, but you need me to
tell me, do you also see
we can end each other's misery

I know

I know it is so wrong
but for you, my heart sings a love song
every time I see you
I know what I need you to do
every time you kiss my skin
I crave your touch all over my body again

Even after

I remember the taste of your lips
the feel of your hands lifting my hips
even after all the lies
I missed the sparkle in your eyes
they say my time I did waste
but I still miss the way you taste
tell me what I should do
because I can't live without you

His touch

His touch turned my skin hot like fire
it caused an untamed desire
I gave him a sly glance
as I slid my hand down his pants
I then beg and plea
for him to make passionate love to me

Fate

I am so tired of everyone
I want to have some fun
let it all come undone
It's just a little crazy
my life has become hazy
everyone is so fake
I desperately need a break
I don't know how much more I can take

My fate

I begged you to let me go
you held on tighter, saying no
my true self has begun to fade
my bed I have made
myself I need to find
the self I've left behind
maybe it is too late
this is my fate

Be free

The older I get
the more I seem to forget
everything I have been through
the people I once knew
the ones that are now dead
their faces still enter my head
I remember all they said
my soul I have sold
I have become withdrawn and cold
why won't they leave me be
I want to be free
Free to be the real me

Falling

I sit alone all night and cry
I do not understand why
all I know is how I feel
these self-inflicted wounds won't heal
I twist it up inside
every time I gain balance, I slide
I can hear everyone calling
yet I still keep falling

Not today

Everyone is out for their gain
no wonder we are all insane
life is just a twisted game
it's full of lies and shame
they say this isn't true
wanting to brainwash you
let us all stand up and say no
we won't do as you say

not today

Do you

Do you ever feel like you're outside looking in
waiting to be found once again
like no one knows the real you deep inside
there is no one in which you can confide
like you don't belong in this place
you exist somewhere between time and space
do not worry if you do
I feel this way, too

why

Why are you so afraid
Afraid of the connection we have made
why won't you answer me
I call out to thee
everything I say is true
perhaps it's too much for you
go ahead and continue to hide

it won't change how you feel inside

Give me

Give me something to believe in
in this world full of lies and sin
give me something real
that I can touch and feel
something that won't tear me apart
something that will touch my heart

Change

Is it too late to set it all straight
to change our fate
to go and fight for what we know is right
our lives, we could rearrange
our destructiveness, we can change

please don't give up on me
can't you see
I would be in sheer misery

Precious destiny

To me, you held out your hand
by your side, I now stand
like birds of a feather
we should always be together
I crave your firm lips
your hand on my hips

I know you also crave me
your precious destiny

Feel

It cannot be real

this way, I've come to feel
I am so lost inside
my grip on reality has begun to slide
so, stab me with a knife
bring me back to life
make me feel
make me real
my heart forever remains
you can have all the blood in my veins
come and take it from me
End my eternal misery

Dark prince

The dark Prince has come
darkness and death are where he's from
nothing can be done

he's come for the innocent one
she is the final key
to fulfill his destiny
she is drawn into his arms
unable to resist his charms
for him, she gives up her wings
and all other pure things

The Innocent

She was so innocent and pure
yet still so very unsure

set out to find her destiny
she longed to be free
this she would defend
this desperate to blow like the wind
from place to place
against time, she must race
until she finds where she belongs
and fixes all her wrongs

Your wish

Your wish is my command
reach out, take my hand
and the darkness you no longer shall hide

fill me deep inside
let me take away your pain
the pain that drives you insane
in me, you can confide
I will stand by your side
trust in me
I will end your misery
I shall remove the knife
bringing you back to life

Inside

This is how I feel inside
I feeling I no longer wish to hide
There is so much that needs to be said

I feel so dead
dark thoughts flow through my head
can you handle all I have to say
if so you're welcome to stay
if not, walk away
my soul is tattered and worn
my heart is lost and torn
the moment I was born
my death, I knew no one would mourn
I am the one you cannot see
the one that is pain and misery
the one that makes this world spin
the seer of all sin
this is me
a soul that shall never be free

so mote it be

You are so unique
your soul I seek
I am your destiny
I call out to thee
look deep within; you shall see
you belong to me
I belong to you, too
there's nothing we can't do
give in to your fate
before it's too late
I am inside your head
listen, and you will hear all I've said
the one that catches you as you fall
listen, you shall hear my call
I'm the voice inside your head
the one that awakes you from the dead
so much I can make you feel
your dreams, I can make real
answer my call come to me
let me set you free
so mote it be

My addiction

It's so hard for me to deal
I don't know how I feel
this emptiness inside of me can't be real
why won't my old wounds heal
I feel the darkness all around

to my addiction, I am bound
I have become its slave
it wants to send me to my grave

Fate

why do you run from destiny
give in to it be free
to be you deep inside

to no longer have to hide
tell the world what you feel
know what is truly real
show them you refuse to fall
you're in it for the long haul
you're not afraid to love or hate
you're ready to accept your fate
before it is too late

Untitled

In your eyes, I can see all your pain and misery
in your eyes, I see your fears
let me kiss away your tears
in your eyes I see the raging flame

it lurks beneath the shame
shame from your dark past
the happiness that never lasts
fighting a battle, you may never win
trying desperately not to give in again
let me be the escape you need
your heart and soul, I can feed
I can set you free
if you just let me

Do you believe

Do you believe two souls that have never met
can reach out and connect
that they can find a balance between

even though each other they have never seen
that they can feel each other's pain from deep inside
Their desperation to hide
feel each other's souls cry out to theirs
as their heart continues to tear
Tear from the pain deep in their heart
even if they are miles apart
it has happened to me, you see
it's a gift I did receive
so, I myself do believe

That Chance

In the past, so many mistakes were made

To take a chance, you are now afraid
You have given up the chase
Hiding in your safe place
Fear is buried deep inside
Causing you to continue to hide
Yet your soul is aching to be free
Crying out to your unknown destiny
Destiny hears this call
As you still refuse to fall
Let go of your doubts!
To your soul, your fate shouts
Come to me
Or bring me to thee
I will it so shall it be
Forcing you to give yourself to me
Your sweet-twisted up destiny.

Forget

Born from that which is dark
In this world, she shall leave her mark
Like lightning, your heart she will hit
Become the one you can never forget
She is the one with so much regret
Feeler of people's pain she's never met
The one you can show your true self to
The one that would love you for you

She

She sits in her home all day.
She never says the things she needs to say
She is everyone's crutch
Deep inside her, there is so much
So much more than they realize
For her age, she is uniquely wise
She is an old soul who was reborn
Between both realms, she is torn
Around her heart, there is a wall
Yet, in others' eyes, she can see all
See their inner fears
Taste their salty tears
Feel their deepest desire
It burns her soul like fire

Nothing is Fair

Nothing in life is genuinely fair
Pain and sorrow we all have our share
We all tried desperately not to care
Yet our human feelings get in our way
Forcing us to continue to stay
We are forever trapped here
Trapped inside our endless pain and fear

Our Love

Our love was real, and it shall forever remain
Not being together will drive us insane
Each other we shall never forget
Being with you, I could never regret
You are the love of my life
In my heart, I'll always be your wife
Even if we say goodbye
The love we share will never truly die

Feelings

Fillings: what are they
I want mine just to go away
Why let them flow
No, mine I now refuse to show
I have become the one
That shall show none
The one that keeps them inside

Only in myself, will I confide
Forget all the tears I should have cried
Forget the soft side
It has died
I am who I am; to let that change,
I will be damned
Go ahead and stare
See if I care
Your touch makes me cringe
All I want now is revenge
Vengeance for all the stuff you did
For all the things you hid
The day I hear you have died
It shall be the day I'm satisfied
When I spit on your grave
Take back all that I gave
Know that I am the one that put you there
That atlas I no longer care

I Feel

This is what is real
This is what I feel
Trapped inside this cage
All I feel now is intense rage
The world I shall shake
Your will to live I will take
The one to take your breath
To cause your untimely death
My true self is forever unseen
I have become withdrawn and mean
I have become the seeker of pain
I am now wholly insane

Untitled 2

Never-ending darkness all around.
I am lost, never again to be found
Then, there was the twisting of fate
It's not too late, not too late
Come here to me, my tempting destiny
Is it you, or is it me
Fighting against time and space
Desperate to find our one true place
Twisting, turning, yearning, burning

Set me free, or just let me be
We are each other's destiny
Torch me, scorch me, let me feel anything
Bleeding, screaming, take me
Break me, set me free
My fiery destiny

It is too Late

It is too damn late; it came too late
The hell with our fate
I now make my way
I am here to stay
Never, ever go away
Indeed, I cannot go away
Yet, honestly, I can never really stay
Let us cry
Let us lay here in this hell and die
Let me fly to where all mankind belong
Never mind it is already gone

Meaningless Gain

Endless pain, meaningless gain
Driving this man insane
Desperate to find the peace within
He can't forgive himself for his sin
Death becomes his fear
This death that is so very near
Fighting against all time
He has lost his mind
This man is now hate
This man is now your fate

He can't hide
what he feels inside
Inside, he has already died

Touch

Touch me, my baby
Set my soul free
Touch my blackened heart
Give this tortured man a new start
Give my soul a reason to heal
Give this heart a reason to feel
Kiss me on my frozen lips
Wrap your legs around my hips
Bring this man back to life
Become his wife
Give him your own life

Goodbye

It has been so easy for you to say goodbye
Perhaps these past years have all been a lie
All you do is sigh
As I sit here alone and cry
Here, take this as your little token
It is my heart forever broken
As you sat there and grinned
I told you it was the end
You know that you should be ashamed
I am the only one getting blamed
You know what you did

All the things you constantly hid
Yet you sit here and continue to lie
Your precious high

I Want

I want death to come knocking on your door
I want your stiff body lying on the cold floor
I want your heart to be squeezed
I want your soul to be diseased
I want all your lies to unfold
As your blood runs cold
I want your body to become shaken
As you watch your soul being taken
Taken down to the pits of hell
I want to hear you scream and yell
I would gladly sit in a tiny cell
All I want is to see you fail

You Have

You have taken everything from me.
You are the cause of all my misery
From my hurt, you seek your gain
You are the cause of all my pain
You have the key to my chain
The key is hidden in your black heart
To get the key, I will take you apart
Know that I am coming for you
To stop me, there is nothing you can do
I shall not rest until you are dead
Until I have taken your head
Becoming free of your sin

To finally feel whole once again

Just, Words

Words: what are they
There are so many I could say
Without you, I'd be broken inside
I would have no one in which I could confide
You gave me a new reason to live
To you and only you, my heart, I must give
In your arms, all I feel is happiness
A state of endless bliss
You send me there with just one kiss
What else can I say
In your strong arms, I want to stay
The slightest touch of your hand makes my body shake
My heart and soul become yours to take

Just the tiny brush of your firm lips
Make me want to lift my hips
Wrap my legs around your waist
I begin to beg you for just a little taste
A taste of that sweet bliss
Upon my breast, place a soft kiss
The only time I genuinely rest
Is when I'm lying on your chest
What else must I say or do
To show you that I truly love you

Love and War

Love we all feel it to our core
It is either happiness or war
It can tear you up inside
It can leave the heart petrified
It can nail you right in your heart, Bam
Love isn't worth a damn
Love is one pathetic act
You give, but you never get back
No matter what you give, they want more
It is a never-ending battle and war
They are never satisfied
By how much you have cried
They push, wanting you to break
Your spirit must stay strong, never shake
The question is, how do you feel
When you find out you're the only one who's love is real

They all Ask

They all ask how do you feel
They can't see my heart is now steel
They ask if I will be alright
They don't see I want a fight
They say it is a sin
A sin to hate him
To wish for his death
To want him to take his last breath
He has taken so much for me
why the hell should he remain free
I want it all back
I feel the need to attack
I have this terrible need
To watch him suffer, see him bleed
You asked me how do I feel
I feel the need to kill

He can

Inside my heart and my head
I shall never forget the words he has said
Believing in me, he has changed my destiny
Understanding my desire
He has set my soul on fire
My hunger for life only he can feed
Fulfill my every need

Poison Kiss

They say love is endless bliss
Have they never felt a poisonous snake's kiss
They say love is gentle and kind
Have they never been left behind
They say love shall set the world free
I say it is nothing but sheer misery

Always fighting just to belong
Everything is always going wrong
Perhaps we need a guide
Someone who sees us deep inside
They say this day will come
when we all finally meet someone
Someone who sees us through and through
And the best part is we will see them too
I must disagree. It is nothing but fantasy
No human will ever understand me

Another Day

Everything has come so damn undone.
I have become lost and very numb
Yet, I continue to live
Even when I cannot forgive
Many feelings shall never be told
I have become so damn cold
Talk to me another day
For today
I have no more to say

Never Knew

I never knew the cost
I never knew my soul would become lost
It now belongs to only you
As yours now belongs to me, too
You have become my obsession
I love you with a burning aggression
Cry as you may, go ahead and pout
There will never be a way out
We are each other's destiny
without the other, we will never be free
so come, my love, come to me

Unique

Here I thought I was the only freak
It appears we are both unique
Into my heart, you did creep
while into your bed, I did sneak
There is no way this could go wrong
Together, it's obvious we belong
Come to me, my lover, with your kiss
Together, we'll reach endless bliss

A smile that is

A smile that is like home to me
It makes me weak and tremble in knee
Eyes that see me deep inside
They make me want to no longer hide
A face that heats me to the core
Causing me to always ache for more
Your voice whispers in my head
Remembering all you have ever said
All of this is not worth a damn

When you don't even know who I truly AM

The Distance

In the distance, you hear them all shout
The lights flicker on and then back out
You must always give them your all
Never quit, never fall
The lights on the stage burn hot
You give them all you got
Your soul becomes fused to theirs
It becomes clear how much they all care

In their souls, you plant a seed
As off one another's energy, you feed
In the distance, you hear us, the crowd
We make you strong, make you proud

Sometimes

Sometimes, life does not go as we plan
With what we have, we do what we can
Sometimes, we need something to believe in
Something to bring us back to life again
Sometimes, just blocking them all out
It is so much easier than to scream And shout
Either way, we drink from life's golden cup
We have to fight, never give up
Never run, never hide

We must push all our fears aside

Rock & Roll

In his life of rock & Roll
The lifestyle has taken its toll
The lights of the stage burnt deep in his soul
They never grow dim or dull
Being forever heard is the true goal
For the world to truly understand
He isn't a God, he's just a man

Untitled 3

This fear buried deep inside
causes me to continue to hide
my soul aches to be set free,
crying out to my true destiny
in shadow thick where whispers creep
I tread the path too dark to keep

each heartbeat echoes a haunting plea
to shed the chains and simply be
yet fear keeps drawing me nearer
it becomes agonizingly clear
begging me to merely disappear
you, however, keep drawing me near
especially with that single salty tear
yet shadows whisper soft and low,
reminding me of all I know
in darkness, I find solace in rare
dance without a twisted pair
but in your gaze, a flicker shines
a glimmer of hope that intertwines
with every tear that falls like rain
you pull me back from the edge of pain
in the mirror, I see my reflection
in my eyes, my soul is shouting for connection
yet the constant fear takes over again
remind me of things that have never been
desires I will never feed
I am choking on my own planted seed I
can hear the soul scream
it's like a distant dream
I can see the pain in the eyes
all the discomfort and lies
I can hear the rawness of pain in the voice
it calls me near as if I have no other choice
a soul that is fused to mine
the sounds constant as a wind chime
I'm waiting for the right time
perhaps a perfect lyric or rhyme
in shadows cast our fates intertwine

each whisper echoes a tethered bind
through the chaos, I searched for light.
A melody hidden, veiled from sight
I'll wave the words that break the night
transforming sorrow into flight
for this dance of dark and bright
will find our truth igniting the fight

Tonight

tonight, there may be a glance my way
I will be lost as to what to say
Maybe it will be the one to save me from my terrible misery
tonight, maybe he will touch me
And together, we can reach destiny
overcome this misery
overcome the insanity
a spark ignites within the dark
a whispered promise.
A fragile spark in his gaze
I see my reflection
a chance to break free from this affliction
if our souls collide in the night
we will weave our pain into light
hand in hand, we face the abyss
finding strength and quiet bliss

I see you

I see you
I know what I want to do

I want to kiss you
I want you to kiss my skin
I crave you all over again
In the shadows where our secrets lie
I filled a spark of fire that won't die
each fleeting touch ignites the night
in your embrace, everything feels right
so, let the world fade into the dark
as our hearts dance to an unspoken spark
with every kiss, we defy the pain
in this moment, love will reign again
sharing more than a Cress or a kiss

Meeting of the minds

A meeting of the mind
a moment to stand against time
fighting against all odds and hate
finding one another until it's too late
a love some would call insane

a love with nothing to lose but everything to gain
an obsession that causes death
sealing your fate and stopping your breath
in darkness we will descend
never to be found again
I begged sorrow to let me go
and held on to me shouting no
my true self has begun to fade
my own bed I've undoubtedly made
myself I need to find
the self I've left behind
perhaps it's simply too late
this is my self-created fate.

Shadows of Love

She stands at the edge, where light meets dark,
A fire igniting in the silence, sparking a journey
. With every challenge, she pushes him to rise,
Yet feels the weight of his struggles,
the unspoken cries.
In the depths of his pain, she finds her own,

A mirrored reflection in a heart overthrown.
Together, they dance on the edge of despair,
Yet, in that raw struggle, they find something rare.
Through the storms, they weather, side by side,
Her strength becomes his as they learn to confide.
In the chaos of healing, a bond starts to grow,
Two souls intertwined in the ebb and flow.
So let the rage burn, let the passion ignite,
For in understanding each other, they'll find the light.
Together, they'll rise from the ashes anew,
In the shadows of pain, love will break through
yet will that love be enough to heal
Will it be enough to break the seal
Bringing Lucifer to the surface once more
To help him again soar
Into the wind and light
Out of the darkness of despair and night
A never-ending dispute
A shouting that will never mute
Like the constant playing of his flute

Where shadows creep

In the depths where shadows creep,
Awakening the secrets we keep.
Dance with the demons and face the fight
, In the chaos, we find our light.
Every scar tells a tale,
In the storm, we learn to sail.
Embrace the struggle, don't let it break,
From the ashes, we rise for our own sake.
Time will weather, but we stand tall,
In the end, we'll conquer it all.
Through the fire, through the pain,
We'll find our strength again and again
No matter how tired or weak
That eternal light we continue to seek
Into our true selves, we must peak
Accept all parts, even the inner freak
calmness wash over us like water in a creek
Into the soul, the light will leak
Warming up my frozen cheek
In the depths where shadows creep,
Awakening dreams that we keep
. Embrace the chaos, let it flow,
In the silence, let truth grow.
With every scar, a story told
, Finding strength in the bold.
Through the storm, we rise and stand,
Together, we'll make our final stand
The beauty in life is grand
Fire and drive burning like a brand
Come with me and take my hand

Together we will forever stand
Our voice will echo across the land
Our footprints linger eternally in the sand

This world

In this world, we must leave our mark
Set the stage for others to spark
No matter how tattered and lost
We must infuse ourselves no matter the cost
Take back everything you lost
Seize the moment and melt the frost
The frost that settles in your heart
threatens to rip your soul apart
Burn the bridges and bust the cag
Release the rage

Afraid

They will all be afraid of death
Terrified of taking that last breath
I will be dancing on my grave
Nothing there for them to save
I will know I've given my all
When they were weak, I refused to fall

I do not fear darkness call
In shadows where secrets dwell
, He weaves his dreams,
casting a spell.
Her heartbeat syncs with every note,
A symphony that keeps them afloat.
Together, they dance in the midnight glow,
Embracing the depths where passions flow.
With every lyric, a bond they create,
In the silence of night, they seal their fate.

Ring the bell

Ring that bell,

lift the veil,
rise from hell
Walk out of your cell
Seeker of pain,
friend to the insane
He has played and won the game
Nothing will ever be the same

Chains

Break the chains, embrace the night,
In shadows deep, find your fight.
Echoes of laughter, whispers of dread,
Dance with the demons that swirl in your head.
With fire in your heart and scars to show,
Rise from the ashes. Let your genuine self-glow.
The world may tremble at the path you take,
But in your chaos, a new dawn will break.
We will Split through space and time
Remember our voices like a nursery rhyme,
mimicking the movements like a mime

Tick Tock

Tick, tock, bust that clock,
learn to roll, live to rock.
Kiss that mic
Take that hike
Bust the lock,
suck that cock.
Work those thighs,

make it rise
Bring fire back into those eyes

LUST

The feel of a man's hands on my hips
The taste of my pleasure on his lips
The rise and fall of my chest

The feel of his teeth sliding across my breast
The wild thrust of his hard thorn
So deep when it's loss, I'll mourn
A missing piece of myself That is lost
Leaving me cold as frost
My nails running down his back
My tongue tasting his flesh like a snack
Licking, kissing, tasting, thrusting deep
Making him moan and weep
Pressure building and pulsing like a storm
A deep, unquestionable passion now born
The way our bodies entwine like fire,
Heat rising, igniting every desire.
His breath on my neck, a whisper of need
In this wild dance, we both are freed.
Fingers tracing paths, igniting the skin,
With every touch, the chaos begins.
Lost in the rhythm, hearts racing fast,
A moment like this is too precious to last.
As waves of pleasure crash and collide,
In this sacred space, we both confide.
Together, we soar, two souls intertwined,
In the depths of passion, true bliss we find.

Devour

Devour my body like a beast
Between my parted legs, you feast
I will swallow your thickness whole
While nourishing your very soul
Making you yearn for me is the goal
of passion to passion. Soul to soul
. Exploring the unknown is the goal.
One thing that shouldn't be said.
A thing that's plaguing the thoughts in my head.
If I met, you flesh to flesh instead.
I'd try to seduce myself into your heart and bed.
I wonder what it would be like.
. Like you feeling my skin in place of your mic.
To hear that husky growl in my ear
as I work you like a gear

Depths of Desire

In the depths of desire, where shadows entwine,
Two souls collide, fated by design.
With every whispered secret, we peel back the layers,
Flesh to flesh, igniting the prayers.
Your breath against my skin, like a spark in the night,
Invoking the hunger, a primal delight.
Let's push past the boundaries, break down the walls
, In this dance of seduction, surrender to the calls.
What if I held you close, lost in the heat?
Every heartbeat syncing, our rhythms complete.

To taste every moment, to lose track of time,
In the embrace of this passion, the sublime
Tighten my wrist with rope.
Take me in like dope.
Fuel the fire and feed the demon.
Fill me up with hot semen.
I can take it. I swear
as long as I feel your fingers in my hair

INTENSE

I like things intense.
Anything's better than dull and dense
in your lust, I'd rinse
I like it dirty with a twist of flirty
Those eyes are as blue as the sky
in your arms, I'd love to lie
wrapped up naked under the stars

or in the seat of all your cars
maybe take me in the sand
you will hold my throat, and I your hand
take us both to the promised land
Bite my lip,
from my blood, you sip.
On your flesh, I'll delicately nip
. Licking my way from your jaw to your treasure trail.
I'll give you passion hotter than hell
Is that too much to take in?
The knowledge of my deepest sin?
Is that making you scared?
Now that my lust has flared.
Or is it the net in which you're snared?

Darkness Falls

Darkness falls faster and faster.
Calling out like a slave master
Bending my will and claiming my eyes
Swallowing all excuses and lies

Bleeding my veins and silencing my cries
On the inside, my soul dies
The reaper smiles and sighs

Winds of time

Knock down all defenses
skin those rawer senses
face the unknown
show what you've never before shown
no longer will you face it alone
let me help you rise above
let me give you a little shove
toss the dime
ride the winds of time

Sanity Shed

This long, drawn-out road has taken its toll.
It has caused a withering in my soul.
There are so many ghosts in my head
. The faces of my loved ones a long time dead.
It makes me regret things that were never said.
This grief was impossible to shed.
My sanity has finally fled.